Dear Parents,

Psalty in Egypt features the extraordinary power of prayer. It shows how God hears us when we pray and how, when we least expect it, prayer can change hearts by removing bitterness and replacing it with love. In the following pages, Psalty the Singing Songbook will teach kids that showing God's love, even to our enemies, can change lives.

As with all Psalty products, for this new adventure story, we've chosen struggles and concepts that affect everyone trying to live their Christian faith. We believe that if you learn these concepts as a child, they will stay with you throughout your adult years. And you will be better equipped to live a joyous life, committed to Christ.

Now snuggle close to your little one and follow Psalty; his wife, Psaltina; their booklets Rhythm, Melody, and Harmony; and their trusty dog Blooper on their rewarding adventure in Egypt.

Ernie Rettino and Debby Kerner Rettino

Library of Congress Cataloging-in-Publication Data

Rettino, Ernie, 1949-
    Psalty in Egypt / Ernie Rettino and Debby Kerner Rettino ; design
and illustration by Dale Wehlacz.
        p.   cm.
        "Word kids!"
        Summary : When Psalty's family, visiting Egypt, is kidnapped
by jewel thieves, they are able to prove that prayer and God's love
can change the lives of our enemies.
        ISBN 0-8499-0894-9
        [1. Egypt—Fiction.   2. Robbers and outlaws—Fiction.
3. Christian life—Fiction.   4. Books—Fiction.]   I. Rettino,
Debby Kerner, 1951-   . II. Wehlacz, Dale, 1960-   ill.
III. Title.
PZ7.R32553Pon   1991
[E]—dc20
                                              91-11782
                                                 CIP
                                                  AC

Printed in the United States of America

1 2 3 4 9 RRD 9 8 7 6 5 4 3 2 1

PSALTY in EGYPT

Characters and Story by
Ernie Rettino and Debby Kerner Rettino

Design and Illustration by
Dale Wehlacz

WORD
Kids!

WORD PUBLISHING
Dallas·London·Vancouver·Melbourne

"Welcome Psalty and family!" Akeem, the head of the Cairo Museum, shook Psalty's hand.

"Hello, Akeem!" answered Psalty. "Thank you for inviting my family to see your new discovery."

"We can't wait!" added Rhythm. "Just think, ancient Egyptian treasures!" said Harmony.

"They must be very valuable," said Melody.

"Yes, we must keep the treasure guarded at all times," warned Akeem. "Robbers might try to steal it."

"When can we see the treasure?" asked Rhythm eagerly.

"Right away! Let's take my Jeep," offered Akeem. "Our dig* is in the shadow of the Great Pyramid*."

As they approached the Great Pyramid, they could see the famous Sphinx*.

"This way," said Akeem as he led them past the guards and through a dark tunnel. Rhythm heard a noise. Was someone behind them?

"I thought I heard someone following us," said Rhythm nervously.

"You're hearing things in the dark," laughed Harmony.

Finally the tunnel emptied into a large room filled with fantastic treasure!

There were golden plates and cups covered with jewels. There were chairs and tables and a boat. Jewelry made of gold and silver and precious gems were heaped all over. The booklets had never seen anything like it!

"I see why robbers would like to get their hands on this!" said Psalty.

"What was that?" Rhythm jumped. He heard a sound, but nobody else heard anything. "I think the flickering light is making you jittery," soothed Psalty.

But Rhythm *had* heard something. Hiding in the shadows, waiting to steal the treasure, were robbers! They had found a secret entrance to the treasure room.

"Come, my friends," said Akeem. "Tomorrow you can help as we begin listing the treasure for the museum. Now let's see some of the other sights of Egypt."

Akeem led Psalty and his family back through the dark tunnel to the entrance. The robbers quickly grabbed the three biggest jewels . . .

then hurried back through the secret passage. They got outside before the others and hid the jewels on the headdresses of some nearby camels.

"Oh, Dad! Camels!" squealed Melody, as the family came out of the tunnel. "Can we go for a camel ride, please?"

"That would be fun," agreed Psaltina.

Psalty and his family got on the bumpy camels and rode into the desert.

The Pyramids looked so big from the family's desert view.

Suddenly, two robbers in flowing dark robes galloped up. They grabbed the reins of the booklets' camels and raced off across the sand. Psalty and Psaltina tried to chase them, but the robbers were too fast. The booklets had been kidnapped!

The booklets were really scared. "Where are you taking us?" demanded Harmony.

"Be quiet! You are very noisy booklets," one of the robbers shushed them. "You see the jewels your camels are wearing? We stole them from the treasure!

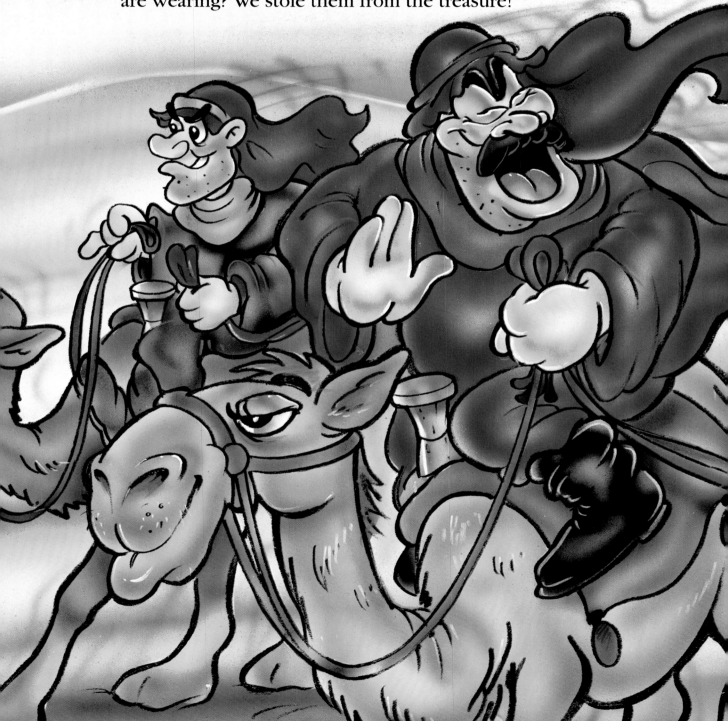

Now we are going to sell them to a smuggler and get lots of money. You just happened to be on the wrong camels. Ha, ha, ha! Maybe we can get some money for you, too!"

The poor booklets didn't know what to do. They didn't like these mean robbers at all!

The only thing they could do was pray. *"Dear Lord, You are a great God, and we need Your help. Please save us from these mean robbers and take us back to our parents. In Jesus' name, Amen!"*

The booklets had been riding a long time. They were hot, thirsty, and tired. Sand was getting in their pages and they were feeling itchy!

"Look!" said Melody. "There is an oasis* ahead of us!"

The oasis had shady palm trees and a spring of cool water. What a welcome relief from the hot desert sand!

The bad robbers dragged the booklets off their camels. They rudely shoved them into an old nomad's* tent. "Don't let these booklets get away," the robber told the old man.

"Ah, guests. How nice! Please sit down and have some dates and goat's milk." Melody, Harmony, and Rhythm were very confused. First they had been kidnapped, and now they were being offered good food!

"Why are you being so nice to us?" Melody asked.

"To my people, a stranger is an honored guest," exclaimed the old man. "Tell me, what brought you to my tent?"

"Those bad men stole jewels from the treasure. Then they kidnapped us!" huffed Harmony.

"Ah," sighed the old nomad. "My nephews are still up to their old tricks."

"Your nephews?" gasped Melody.

"Yes. I keep hoping they will get honest jobs, but they choose to do bad things no matter what I say to them." The old man looked down sadly.

"Why don't we pray for the robbers?" suggested Rhythm.

"Pray for those awful men? You must be kidding!" Harmony couldn't believe what Rhythm was saying.

"Maybe Rhythm is right," offered Melody. "They have been mean to us, but God might help them change."

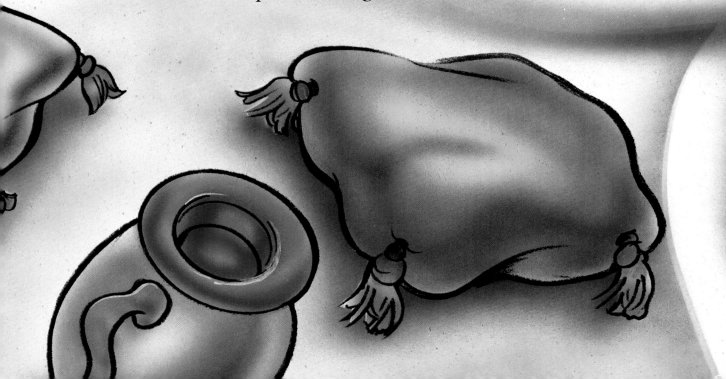

Rhythm prayed: "*Dear Lord, please help the robbers change their bad ways. And show them how much You love them. Help them to start living for You. In Jesus' name, Amen.*"

The old nomad had tears in his eyes. "Thank you for praying for my nephews," he said gratefully. "Nobody has ever cared about them before."

The robbers burst into the tent and dragged the booklets to their feet. "We sent a ransom* note to your parents. They will meet us at the Cairo marketplace. If they bring us enough money, we'll let you go. Ha, ha, ha! We will get money from selling the jewels and money for you, too."

The robbers were very pleased with themselves.

"You don't have to be so mean," Rhythm protested.

"What are you talking about?" asked one robber roughly.

"God loves you, and He wants to be friends with you," added Harmony.

"That's right," Melody added. "God will forgive you and give you a new start if you'll ask Him."

"Be quiet!" ordered a robber. "I don't want to hear talk like that. Let's go!"

The old nomad waved sadly from the door of the tent. Then the robbers and the booklets headed back out across the desert sand.

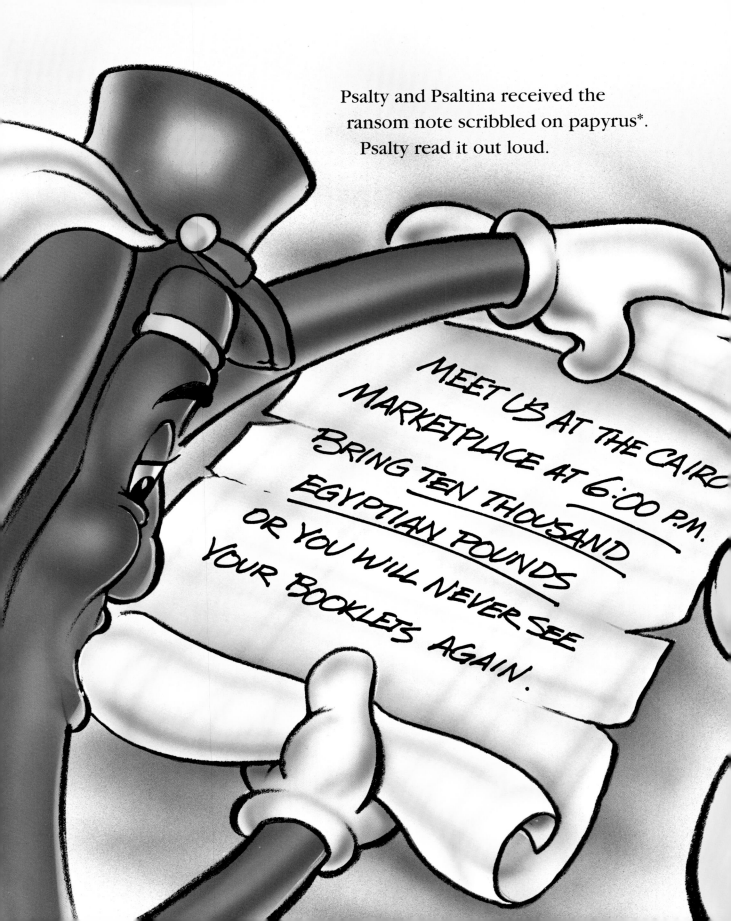

Psalty and Psaltina received the ransom note scribbled on papyrus*. Psalty read it out loud.

"What should we do?" asked a very worried Psaltina. "Those awful men have our booklets!"

"I will inform the police!" announced Akeem.

"Let's pray for the robbers," said Psalty. Praying was all they could do.

Out in the desert Melody tried again. "You don't have to be criminals," she said. "God loves you, and He wants you to be His friend."

"If you don't be quiet, I'll put a gag* on you!" answered a robber roughly.

"God STILL loves you!" Melody insisted.

"We have been mean to you. Why are you being so nice to us?" asked one of the robbers.

"Because God loves us," answered Rhythm. And we show His love to others by being nice—even to people who are mean to us."

"I can't stand this any more!" said one robber. "Do you think God really loves me? Even after all the bad things I've done?"

"Yes," Melody quickly answered. "God will forgive anything if you are really sorry." The Robbers began to feel sorry for all the mean things they had done.

"I want to be friends with God, just like you booklets," said one robber.

"Me, too," said the other robber. "I am going to stop doing bad things and be nice. We'll start by taking you back to your parents."

"Hooray!" shouted the booklets. "Praise the Lord!"

Soon the booklets and the robbers arrived at the Cairo
marketplace. Blooper barked loudly when he saw them.
Psalty, Psaltina, and Akeem rushed over to the booklets.
They were so glad to see them!
The police grabbed the robbers.
"Wait!" cried Rhythm. "The robbers have changed."
"It's true, Mom and Dad!" said Harmony.

"At first we were afraid because they were mean to us," added Melody. "But we prayed for them. Then God filled our hearts with His love for these men."

"Here are the jewels we stole," the tall robber said to Akeem. "We are very sorry. To make it up to you, we will work for free at the museum."

Psalty talked to Akeem and the police. "I think these men deserve another chance," he said. Everyone agreed.

Akeem, Psalty and his family, and the two former robbers set off for the museum. God's two new friends were eager to make things right.

Isn't it wonderful what can happen when we pray?

GLOSSARY

Dig (dig) —
A place where scientists dig and uncover valuable old things.

Gag (gag) —
Something put into a person's mouth to keep him from talking or yelling.

Great Pyramid (pir´-ə-mid) —
One of the huge tombs built for a king in Egypt long ago. It is 481 feet high and made of heavy stone blocks. Its four outside walls are shaped like triangles.

Nomad (nō´-mad) —
A tent dweller who moves from place to place.

Oasis (ō-ā´-sis) —
An area in the desert where there is a water well or spring.

Papyrus (pə-pī´-rəs) —
An ancient material on which to write. It is made from the papyrus plant.

Ransom (ran´-səm) —
The price to be paid for the safe return of kidnapped persons.

Sphinx (sfingks) —
A statue creature with the body of a lion and the head of a man. The most famous one is close to Cairo near The Great Pyramid.

THERE'S MORE TO COME! Follow Psalty and family's round-the-world adventures in these other great stories:

PSALTY IN THE SOVIET CIRCUS—a memorized Bible verse brings Psalty comfort when he is mistakenly thrown in jail.

PSALTY IN ALASKA—a snowy dogsled race helps Rhythm learn that we don't have to be afraid of losing if we do our best.

PSALTY IN THE SOUTH PACIFIC—being marooned on a South Seas island shows Harmony how trouble can help us grow.

PSALTY ON SAFARI—an exciting game-show win and a trip to Africa show Melody that helping with God's work can be more exciting than spending money on herself.

PSALTY IN AUSTRALIA—a vacation "down under" gives Psalty's family a glimpse of God's amazing creativity and reminds them that God has a unique plan for everyone.